THE BOULDER BROTHERS

Meet Mo and Jo

A JUMP • INTO • CHAPTERS Book

Text Copyright © 2014 Sarah Lynn Scheerger
Illustrations Copyright © 2014 Pierre Collet-Derby
All rights reserved/CIP data is available.
Published in the United States 2014 by
🍎 Blue Apple Books, 515 Valley Street,
Maplewood, NJ 07040
www.blueapplebooks.com
Printed in China
First Edition 11/14

Hardcover ISBN: 978-1-60905-501-1
Paperback ISBN: 978-1-60905-561-5

2 4 6 8 10 9 7 5 3 1

Does Mo smell better?

Mo sniffs. Jo sniffs. The stink is still there!

Is Mo right about Jo?

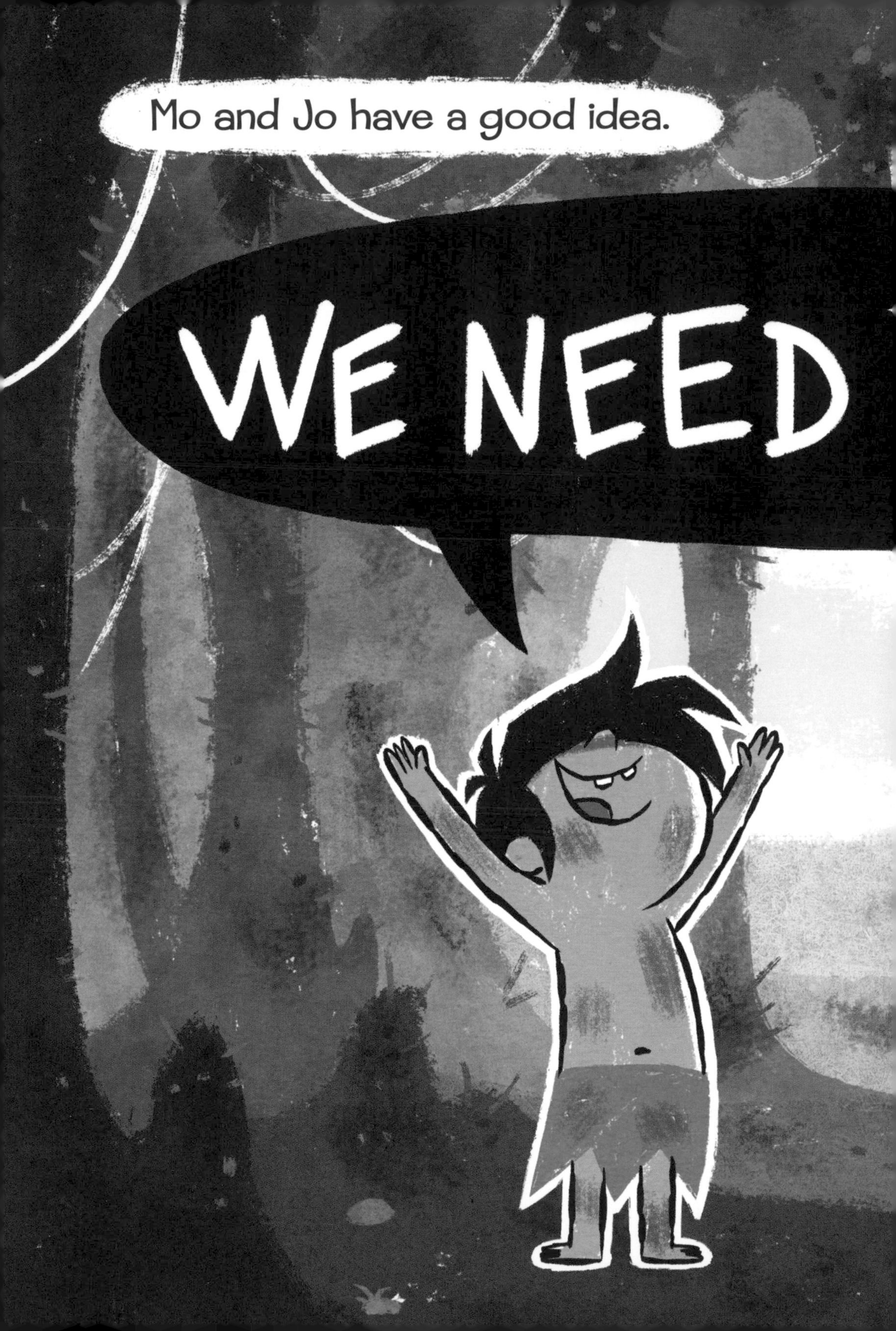
Mo and Jo have a good idea.
WE NEED

Mo and Jo have not
had a bath in a long time.

Jo smells good. Mo smells good.
But the stink is not gone.

They find out what stinks.

Mo and Jo know what to do.

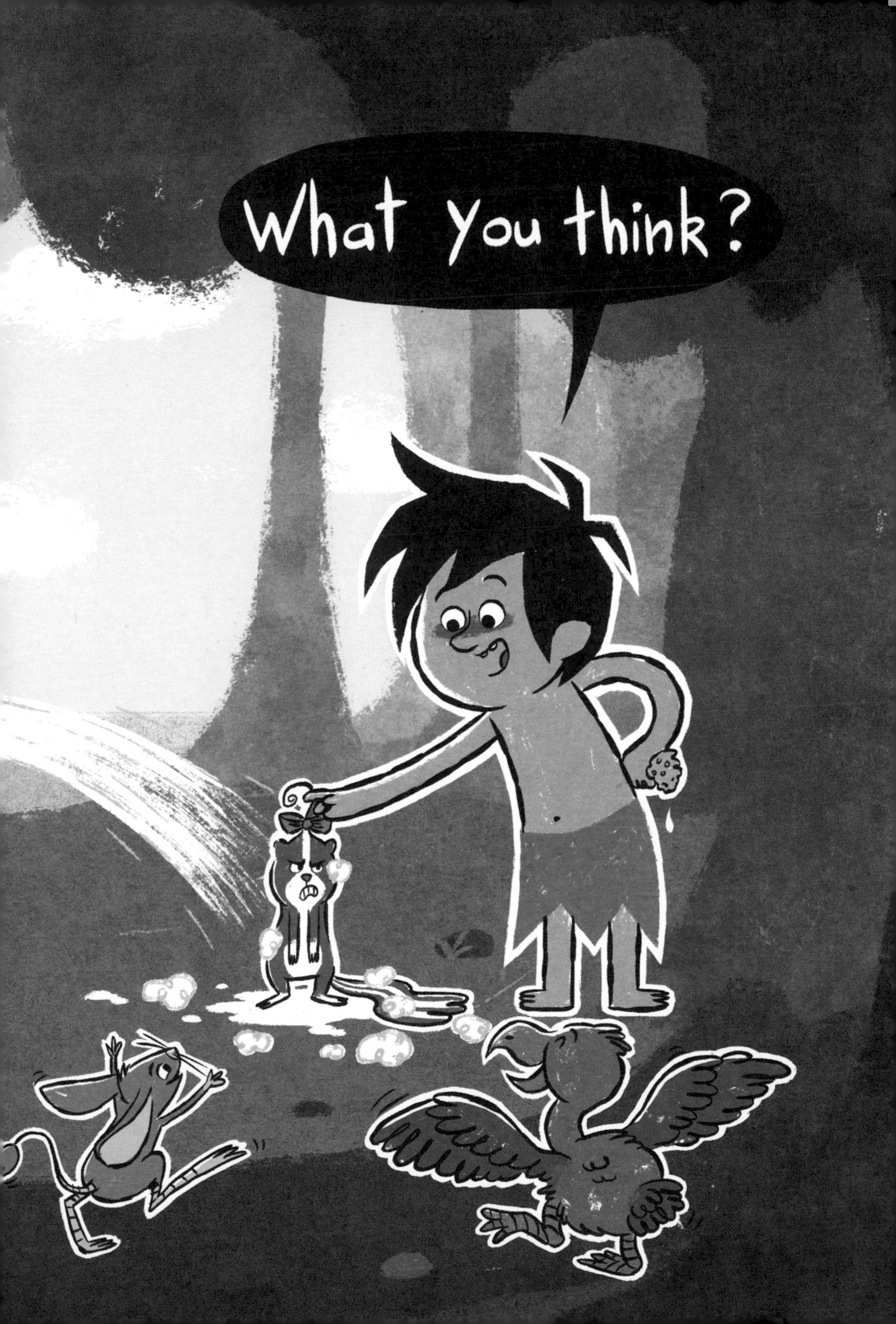
What you think?

The skunk liked the stink.
Can Mo and Jo run faster than the skunk?

CHAPTER 2:
HiDE AND PEEK!

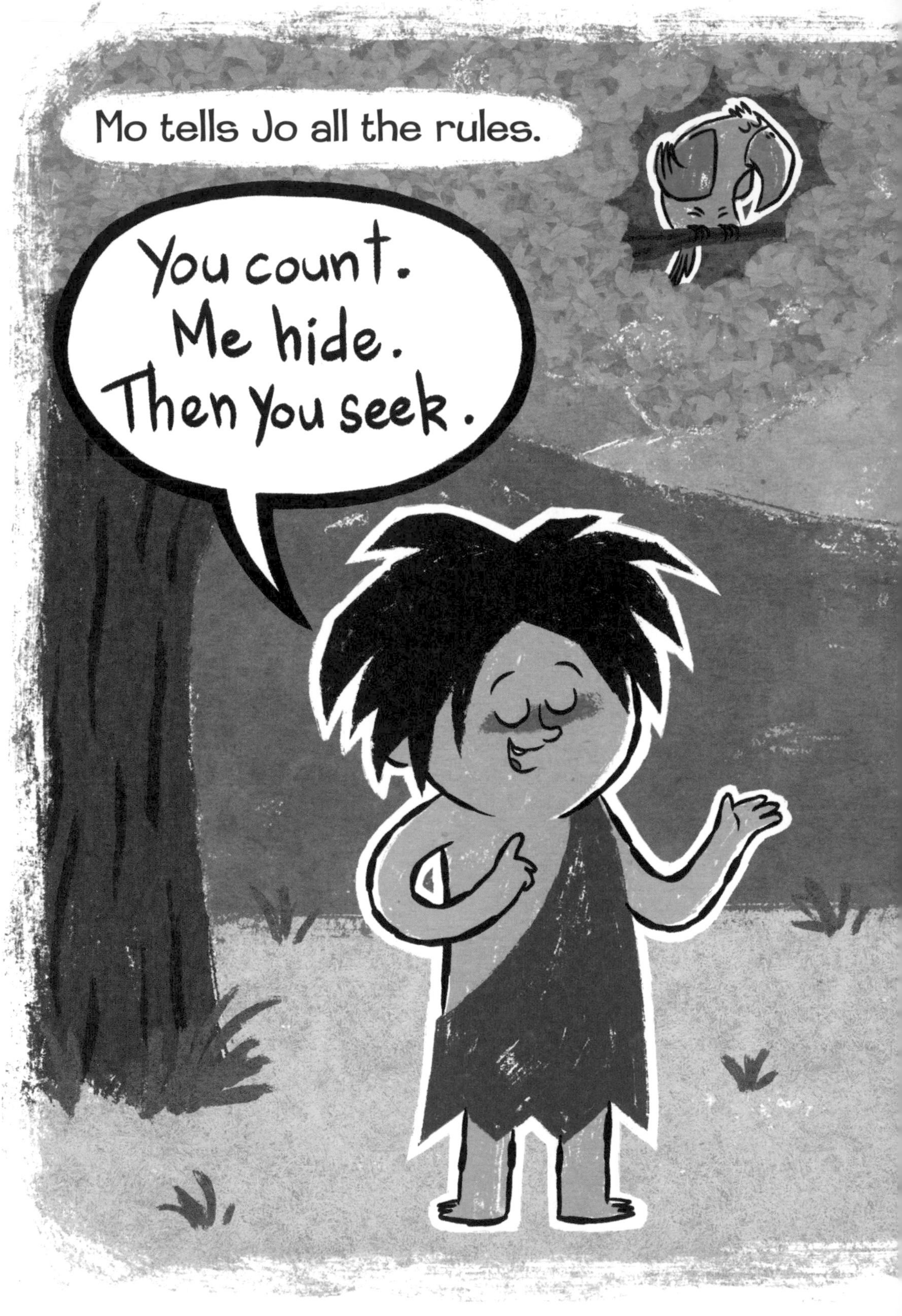
Mo tells Jo all the rules.
You count. Me hide. Then you seek.

Mo finds a hiding place.

1. 2. 3.
4. 5. 6. 7.
8. 9. 10.